LEARN TO

DETECTIVE DAN

and the

Puzzling Pizza Mystery

written and illustrated by
Timothy Roland

ZondervanPublishingHouse
Grand Rapids, Michigan
A Division of HarperCollinsPublishers

Detective Dan and the Puzzling Pizza Mystery
Copyright © 1993 by Timothy Roland

Requests for information should be addressed to:
Zondervan Publishing House
Grand Rapids, Michigan 49530

Library of Congress Cataloging-in-Publication Data

Roland, Timothy.
    Detective Dan and the puzzling pizza mystery / Timothy Roland.
      p. cm.
    Summary: Detective Dan solves the case of the missing pizza and,
with the aid of a Bible verse, helps Bernard understand why he
should not tell lies to his friends.
    ISBN 0-310-38101-0 (pbk.)
    [1. Pizza—Fiction. 2. Parties—Fiction. 3. Honesty—Fiction.
4. Christian life—Fiction. 5. Mystery and detective stories.]
I. Title.
PZ7.R6433Di   1993
[E]–dc20   93-3496
                                                                             CIP
                                                                             AC

Edited by Dave Lambert and Leslie Kimmelman
Interior and cover design by Steven M. Scott
Illustrations by Timothy Roland

Printed in the United States of America

93 94 95 96 97 98 / CH / 10 9 8 7 6 5 4 3 2 1

To those who call me uncle:
Andrew, Beth, Joshua, Matthew,
Malachi, Stephanie, Janet,
Takoda, Kessiah, and . . .

CONTENTS

Chapter One
THE MISSING PIZZA

I am Detective Dan.

I like to solve mysteries.

I also like to eat.

One day I was waiting
to go to Bernard's pizza party.
I looked at my Bible verse
for the week.

Keep your tongue from
evil and your lips
from speaking lies.
Psalm 34:13

It was an easy verse to remember.
But it was not always easy to obey.
Suddenly I felt the ground shake.
"Help! Help!" cried a voice.
I looked up and saw Bernard
running toward me.

"My pizza is missing!"
Bernard yelled.
"Now there will be nothing to eat
for my party!"
"Tell me about the pizza," I said.
"I bought it this morning,"
said Bernard.
"Then what happened?" I asked.
"I put the pizza on a table
in my backyard," Bernard replied.

"I cut the pizza.
Then I went inside.
When I came out,
the pizza
was gone!"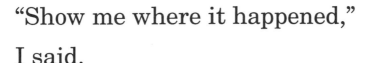
My stomach growled.
"Show me where it happened,"
I said.
Bernard ran toward his house.
I whistled for my dog, Newton.
He did not come.
He had been missing all morning.
He had even missed lunch.
It was a mystery.
But I did not have time
to look for him now.
I had a case to solve.

I put on my detective coat.

I ran after Bernard.

He does not run very fast.

Soon we met Mandy.

She looked upset.

"My cat, Scarlet, is missing!"

said Mandy.

"So is the pizza," said Bernard.

"The pizza for the party?"

she cried.

"Yes," said Bernard sadly.

"And I just now bought it."

"I thought you bought the pizza
this morning," I said.

Bernard's face turned red.

"Oops!" he said.

"I guess I'm a little confused."

I was confused, too.

Bernard never forgets things
about food.

"There sure are a lot of mysteries,"
said Mandy.
"The pizza is missing.
Scarlet is missing."
"So is Newton," I said.
"Newton?" said Mandy.
"I saw him this morning."
"Where?" I asked.

"He was with Scarlet," Mandy said.

"They ran in this direction."

She pointed.

"That's the way to my house,"
said Bernard, "where the missing
pizza was last seen."

My stomach growled again.

I was hungry to solve this case.

Chapter Two
PIZZAS DON'T FLY

I followed Bernard to his backyard.
"Here is where the pizza was,"
he said.
I looked on top
of the empty picnic table.
I looked under it.

But there were no clues.

Not even a single crumb.

What a strange case, I thought.

"This is what I used to cut the pizza,"
said Bernard.

He held up a knife.

It was covered with red sauce.

"How many pieces did you cut?"
I asked.

"Uh—six," Bernard said slowly.

"One for each person I invited."

"Who is coming?" I asked.

Bernard said, "You and Mandy,
Tara, Carmen, and—and Farley."

"I do not think Farley is coming,"
said Mandy.

"I just saw him running
toward the park.

He had a box in his hand."

"A box," I said slowly.

"Was it the size of a pizza?"

"I think so," said Mandy.

"It's my missing pizza!"

yelled Bernard.

I ran to the gate.

Then I thought about Farley.

I did not want to face him alone.

I whistled
for Newton.
But Newton
did not come.
I looked back
at Bernard
and Mandy.
"Come on,"
I said.

"Where are you going?"
asked Bernard.

"To solve the case," I replied.

"But it is already solved,"
Bernard said.

"Farley took the pizza.

And he probably ate it."

My stomach growled.

"We do not know that for sure,"
I said.

"It had to be him,"
said Bernard firmly.
"I saw him sneaking around here
this morning."
"Why didn't you tell me
that before?" I asked.
Bernard's face turned red again.
"I forgot," he said.

I ran out of the yard.

Mandy followed.

Bernard did not.

He sat on a picnic bench.

"What about my party?" he yelled.

 I had
no time
for a party.
I had a case
to solve.

At the park, I saw Farley.

He was holding a box.

It was large and flat.

In his pocket I saw a slingshot.

I had to be careful.

I stepped forward.

Mandy stepped backward.

"What's inside that box?" I asked.

"Something fun," said Farley.

Pizza is fun, I thought.

"Can I see it?" I asked.

"Only if you help me with it,"
said Farley.

I thought about the pizza.

My mouth watered.

"Sure. I will help you," I said.

Farley opened the box.

My mouth
stopped watering.
"That's a kite,"
I said.
"What did you
think it was?" asked Farley.
"A pizza," I said.

Farley laughed. "It would be
pretty hard
to fly a pizza."
Farley was right
about that.

Farley handed me the kite.
"I bought this on vacation,"
he said.
"I just got back this afternoon."
"This afternoon?" I repeated.
"Weren't you over at Bernard's
house earlier today?"
"No," Farley said.
"Are you coming to his pizza party?"
I asked.
"What party?" Farley asked.

Maybe Bernard forgot to invite him,
I thought.
He has been forgetting
lots of things lately.
I held up the kite.
Farley ran with the string.
Soon the kite was in the air.
But my case was still on the ground.

Chapter Three
PIZZA SAUCE

Mandy and I walked back
to Bernard's house.
The walk was quiet.
Bernard's house was not.
Tara was there.

She was wearing a swimming suit
and an inner tube.
"You said you had
a real swimming pool!" she yelled.
"This is a baby pool!"
She kicked the side
of the rubber pool.
Water splashed into the air.
Bernard jumped back.
So did I.

"This is a stupid party!" yelled Tara.

"There's no pizza!

And there's no

real swimming pool!"

Tara grabbed her towel.

She stomped out of the yard.

"You lied, Bernard!" she hollered.

I leaned against the fence.

I thought about my verse

for the week.

Bernard was not careful

with his tongue or his lips.

He had lied

to Tara.

He had lied

about Farley.

Maybe he

had told

other lies, too.

It was hard

to know what

to believe.

Something brushed against my leg.

It was Newton!

Scarlet was with him.

Both were covered with red sauce.

Maybe it is from the missing pizza,
I thought.

It was a juicy clue.

I had to investigate.

"Come here, Newton," I said.

Newton backed away.

He ran out of the yard.

So did Scarlet.

That was strange.

But so was this case.

I ran after Newton and Scarlet.
They stopped behind a food store.
On the ground were some broken
bottles and a puddle of red sauce.
Newton and Scarlet began licking it.

I moved closer.

I sniffed the sauce.

It was ketchup.

I patted Newton's head.

"Sorry," I said.

"I thought you were the pizza thief."

The ketchup
had fooled me.
The case was
still not solved.
I needed
to think.

Chapter Four
A PIECE OF PIZZA

I walked slowly toward
Bernard's house.
Newton followed me.
Scarlet followed Newton.
Something was in the air.
It smelled like pizza.
My stomach growled.

I followed my nose.

It led me into Louie's Pizza Shop.

"Can I help you?" asked a man.

"I am looking for a pizza," I said.

"You came to the right place,"
the man said.

"We make good pizzas. See?"
The man pulled a pizza
from the oven.

He cut it into eight pieces.

"Do you always cut your pizzas
like that?" I asked.

"Yes," said the man.

"Do you want a piece?"

"No, thank you," I said.

"I am looking for a missing pizza.
And you have given me the clue
I need to find it."

I ran to Bernard's house.

Newton and Scarlet followed.

Bernard and Mandy were
in the backyard.

"Scarlet!" yelled Mandy.

"Are you all right?"

"Don't worry," I said.

"It is only ketchup."

Mandy sighed.

She picked Scarlet up
and walked toward the gate.

"Aren't you staying
for the party?"
asked Bernard.

"Sorry,"
said Mandy.

"I have a cat
to clean up."

Bernard sat on a bench.
I stood in front of him
and looked him in the eye.
"Did you buy your pizza at
Louie's Pizza Shop?" I asked.
"Yes," said Bernard.
"Then I think I have
solved the case," I said.

Bernard's mouth dropped open. "You found the pizza?" he asked. "No," I said.

"Because there never was any."

"How do you know that?" Bernard asked. "Because you said you cut

your pizza into six pieces," I said. "But Louie's pizzas are already cut. Into eight pieces."

"Maybe I ordered an uncut pizza," said Bernard.

I picked up the knife from the table.

"Is this what you used
to cut your pizza?" I asked.

"Yes," said Bernard.

I tasted the sauce on the knife.

"Just as I thought," I said.

"It's ketchup."

Bernard's face turned red
one more time.

"All right," said Bernard.

"I lied about getting a pizza."

"But why?" I asked.

"I wanted all of you to like me,"
said Bernard.

"That is why I invited you
to my pizza party.
But I did not have
enough money to buy a pizza.
So I said the pizza was missing."

"You do not make friends by
telling lies," I said.

Bernard looked down.

"I did not think anyone
would find out," said Bernard.

"But I did find out," I said.

"Someone usually finds out
when you lie.

Now you should tell the others
what you did.

And you should tell them you
are sorry."
"I will," Bernard said.
I thought about my verse
for the week:
"Keep your tongue from evil
and your lips from speaking lies."
Bernard had told a lot of lies.
His lies had made
the puzzling pizza mystery messy.
I was happy
that now
he would
clean things up.
But my stomach
was not happy.
It growled.

"You must be hungry," said Bernard.
"I do not have any pizza.

But I make a good peanut butter
and jelly sandwich."
I tried one.
Finally, Bernard was telling
the truth.

THE PUZZLING PIZZA MYSTERY
WRAP-UP REPORT

VERSE FOR THE WEEK:

"Keep your tongue from evil

and your lips from speaking lies."

Psalm 34:13

THE CULPRIT: LYING

Lying is when you try to fool others

by not telling the whole truth.

QUESTIONS TO EXPLORE AND ANSWER:

✔ Why did Bernard lie?

✔ Was that a good reason?

✔ Did Bernard tell more than one lie?

✔ Who did Bernard's lies hurt?

✔ Who have your lies hurt?

✔ What can you do to make things right?

CONCLUSIONS

✔ God does not want us to lie.

✔ Your lies will catch up with you.

✔ Tell the truth!

CASE CLOSED

Detective Dan

Did you enjoy this book about Detective Dan? I have good news—there are *more* Detective Dan books!